To David
Thanks

A Woman's Scorn

Cindy S. Schermerhorn La Comb
2/3/12

A Woman's Scorn

Cindy S. Schermerhorn LaComb

Copyright © 2010 by Cindy S. Schermerhorn LaComb.

Library of Congress Control Number: 2010908482
ISBN: Hardcover   978-1-4535-1940-0
                Softcover   978-1-4535-1939-4
                Ebook   978-1-4535-1941-7

All rights reserved. No part of this book may be reproduced or transmitted in any form or by any means, electronic or mechanical, including photocopying, recording, or by any information storage and retrieval system, without permission in writing from the copyright owner.

This is a work of fiction. Names, characters, places and incidents either are the product of the author's imagination or are used fictitiously, and any resemblance to any actual persons, living or dead, events, or locales is entirely coincidental.

This book was printed in the United States of America.

To order additional copies of this book, contact:
Xlibris Corporation
1-888-795-4274
www.Xlibris.com
Orders@Xlibris.com

*I would like to thank my parents,
Harry and Hattie.
Even though they are no longer here.
My teachers, that made me aware of my passion
for writing, and the persuasion to see it thru.
You know who you are.
My husband Joseph and my children,
Jonas, Cindy & Jacey Jaye
for their support and encouragement.
Mostly for their love and faith.
And the many others that have made this book
possible.*

A WOMAN'S SCORN

A Woman's Scorn tells of a young girl's cruel twist of fate as she grows into womanhood. Born and raised to be her father's son, her rebellion causes her to be locked in a tower. She weeps for her freedom, her life.

Upon the realization that is she is to be a slave to her father's make-believe world, she gives in to his whims until she can escape his madness.

Her father is a doctor and wishes to have a son to follow in his footsteps, to carry on in his stead. He believes that only a son can complete his manhood, make him whole. Her mother died in childbirth; he raises his daughter as a boy, with no care for all that she must endure.

His deep desire for her to be a man becomes his main goal, his obsession. Her young life will never be her own. He trains her as his assistant in his experiments. These experiments sometimes result in death, which her father escapes by taking advantage of the trust of the townspeople, his patients. She feels horrified and guilty, but her father reminds her that a man has no room for weakness.

Upon her father's death, she is filled with hope as she starts a new life. Little by little, she learns the ways of a woman until she finds her true love. She is happy, but not for long. Her man turns out to be a maniac who will have every woman he comes across. She is enraged, and for the first time, she is thankful for her father who mentored her to kill mercilessly.

When you go from

being the doctor's son

to being the doctor's wife,

from living a suppressed

life to one of

bliss,

then how does it become one

of such horrific cruelty.

Father was a good teacher.

I have been an excellent student.

And until now, nobody knew . . .

PART ONE

CHAPTER
ONE

S HE WAS STABBED with the dull blade of guilt, wielding a deep gash into her heart, also penetrating deeply into her soul.

She moped about listlessly without a shred of life left in her being – a lost spirit, nothing more than a lost dark entity.

How could she have been so cold, so calculating? And have remained so calm? How could she ever have possessed such cruelty? Even though she knew her father had taught her well. It had to be done.

Deep within, way down deep, the darker side was hidden away, just waiting to be used. And somehow she had found it, summoned it for her very own use to suit her urgent need.

But, now disbelieving, with only the throbbing ache of guilt twisting her emotions, she knew it had happened. Yes, she was the one who had committed this inhumane act.

Earlier, she knew it had to be done, but who could do it? Surely not her. Though it was what she had wanted. Sweet revenge. No one else could give her the satisfaction she desired. So, with nowhere else to turn, with all this burning rage boiling in her veins, she knew she had to find it in herself to be the one capable of doing this heinous, unspeakable crime. Yes, it was within her to do this. Way down deep. Still it was there, and she had to allow herself to do this. Fed by rage, she thought this just a simple task.

It was finally over.

But was it? Oh no! Not for her, for now she really no longer existed as she had known herself. No, that version of her had been replaced with the dark emptiness of sorrow. She became nothing more than a ghost of herself. All she had done, the great struggle to become herself, to prove herself, to be the *she* she wanted to be. Gone. Gone.

Her body – was fine, though limp and almost motionless, as if time and space were moving without her.

Her mind – an emotional mess that could not be sorted by the twisting and churning thoughts that guilt just would not let untwine, which only prevented any chance of relief or escape. It would always be there.

Her spirit, her soul – would be something to be pitied, perhaps. No longer could it ever soar again the way it once had. No way could it ever be lifted to the heights it had known before. It would only be suspended in space and time, with nowhere to go, with no want to be or exist. Forever to stay in this place, the scene, as it seemed to continually play over and over, again and again in her mind. So it too would never escape, for it had also been trapped by guilt.

What could she do? With no possible escape, she could only wish to disappear, dissolve into nothingness. For her, this too would be impossible. This was worse than death could ever be. Death, for her, would be much too kind and an invited welcome relief, which was not to be granted.

She had to be, and always would be, reminded of her darker self, of her wicked, treacherous ways, of the evil she had called upon from within herself that she possessed. It was no longer hidden and had been used. Yes, she had definitely used it.

But she had to keep this promise. She had to keep the promise to herself. Yes, she did want revenge, and indeed, she had her revenge.

Now, she would only be a sorrowful mourner of her own piteous guilt. It would now and forever surround her entire being. She knew there was no help, no escape, no relief. No, she knew this was exactly what she deserved.

Why had they put her in such a predicament? Why had they made her feel this way, to lead her to such atrocities?

Why couldn't her father just accept her for who she was? For what she was? Why couldn't he just love her? Teach her the good in life. Why couldn't they leave her husband alone? Why couldn't the world just leave her be? she thinks.

But none of that was meant to be, and now it was too late. Too late to think how she could have done it differently. Too late to change anything. Too late to realize just how she would feel once her revenge had been exacted.

The hideousness was over, to leave her forever tormented.

She knows what she has done and will live with this knowledge till the end of her time. And she knew no one would ever believe it, that never, never will even the greatest minds of the future believe or imagine that it was I . . .

She sits in the dingy, dirty little space that is called her room. It wasn't much to look at; in fact, she hated being locked in here. One room in the upper tower. Nothing but dirt and dust everywhere. A small bit of mat for bedding and an old rag for a blanket. The only furniture was a mirror and a small stool. The only nice thing about the room was a little oval window, other than the fact it looked out over the rubbish-filled alley.

Staring wide-eyed at her image in the dusty mirror was a young woman of barely fourteen just beginning to blossom into womanhood. But who would know? The image staring back was wrapped in tight bandage; hair cut so short, and the dullest color of brown; big rounded shoulders; wide hands; and very fat fingers. Here sits the son her father never had.

Her whole life, since early childhood, she was daddy's little boy. She remembers her father's constant praise. "You are a good boy, you are a strong boy. You will make me a proud papa when you are grown, just like I did for my papa." He told me that the greatest honor that could be bestowed upon a man was for him to have a son, and for that son to follow in his footsteps. "I did that for my father. You will do that for me." From that moment in her life, she knew she would never be the girl her mother gave birth to, but would always be daddy's little boy until she was grown. Many times she had wondered, what then? How will she ever grow to be the person she was supposed to be, and who will she be? Now, she thinks she should have known what he had in store for her.

He was this dreary little town's doctor. He was all they had, and they believed in him. But ha, if they only knew the things she knew, the things he had taught her early on. He had said every great doctor must know these things. He taught her that his son would have to learn all his methods in his practice to be a great doctor such as himself, but more importantly, she would have to know these things in life to carry with her always, and to never forget all he had taught her.

He had done all that his father had taught him, and it had helped him in all aspects of his life. Someday she too would be thankful for all he had thus far taught her and all he would continue to teach. Yes, he was their much-adored doctor; they all greatly respected him. They continued their visits with him even when they seemed better. He had told them he would have to keep track of their progress to be sure they were indeed getting better. Their trust for him kept them going back to him, their belief in him. Yes, if they only knew that they, as patients, were truly the great doctor's experiments. With patients silenced by anesthesia, you could learn a lot about the human body, do a lot to the human body; with the hope of medicines making them well again, most would never know.

Her mother had died after giving her life, with each never seeing the other. How she had longed for a mother, for her mother. A mother's love could have made all the difference in the world to her. It could have changed things for her. Now and then. But to be raised by dear Dad alone, it had to be. She never knew quite how to be a girl. Not ever, besides assisting with female patients did she see any other females. None of them even knew – to them they thought and believed she was the doctor's son. He had taught her all about how to be a boy, dress like a boy, and do the work of a man. Now, how was she ever to learn how to be a woman?

She memorized all that she heard of the patients' jabber and gossip, the things they would tell her father. Hoping to learn whatever she could to make this journey into womanhood. *Yes, Father I am a good student.* She thinks if he only knew . . . Yes, she knew little, but someday she would learn. She would have to, wouldn't she?

He has taught her to think as, to act as, and to be a boy. Now believing she was becoming a young man, he was ready to teach her the things every adolescent boy should know – the woman's body, how it worked, but mostly, how it worked to satisfy man.

After all the boyhood chores, all the fetching, all the cleanups, all the disposing of body parts, gallons of blood, bodies, and all of her father's failed attempts at healing, mending, creating, and exploring. Now, Father said it was time to be a real assistant, be at his elbow at all times. It was time to become a man.

At this point in life, every female patient was to become the instrument of education to the young son. The doctor would convince each one how important it was for him to allow his assistant to help them undress. He had taught his son well. Next, to have them lie down on the cold sterile examining table, a table as cold and sterile as the doctor himself. The room was just as cold with only the hope of its sterility. White, but dimly lit, except the bright light that shone down from above the table into the eyes of the patients. The assistant would slip the ether over their mouths, and they would be out cold before they knew it.

That is when it began. The simple touching, caressing, stroking, kissing, nibbling, and yes, even biting. Father was teaching it all.

Yes, Father was teaching it all. She did not understand why this seemed important for Father to be teaching his young son. She felt Father would never give the opportunity for her as male or female to ever go out into the world on her own. She knew he would keep her there at his beck and call throughout his entire life. She knew that as long as he lived, she would never be free. So why is he teaching her in the ways of men? How to be a man – where other than here would she ever get to experience any of it? She did not approve of his teachings and did not like the lessons any better. She still felt she was not learning what a man liked. She now was only learning how a man could please a woman. She did not understand how this would help her later in life as Father insisted it would. She did know that with every lesson she was taught, Father seemed thrilled and excited as he watched her perform each lesson as he had demonstrated.

Next was the anatomy lesson. Once more, the female patients would become instrumental to his teaching. He taught his son how to use the scalpel, cutting into the flesh of each patient to teach his son what and where each part was, sometimes even unnecessarily removing organs. "This," he would say, "is a gallbladder. No use, everyone has them. This, my dear son, is the uterus. This is where a woman grows a man his son. Otherwise, it too is useless." He would show how to cut each organ out, saying their names and functions, commenting that most were useless.

Yes, he taught his son how to carve these bodies up with ease. Upon waking, if they did, the great doctor would have grievous explanations as to why it was so urgently necessary to perform surgery on them. He had saved their lives, they were told.

"Take this medicine; you will be well soon." Grateful for this kind act the doctor had performed, they would praise him. After recuperating, they would leave and tell all whom they knew of how the great doctor had saved their lives, never knowing the real purpose. Ah yes, the real purpose, she thinks, if they only knew. For those who did not make it, the doctor would sweetly explain to the families how desperately he tried, only to find nothing could be done. Yes, if only.

CHAPTER TWO

BUT, NOW SITTING here, knowing her father believes he had done all he can do for his growing son, she cries. She had tried so hard to make him understand, to make him see. She is not his son. She herself had been convinced for a very long time. The whole part of her childhood, all that she had been told, all she had been taught, all Father had promised her to come – didn't and, she knew, wouldn't. She was a good student; she had to have learned something of herself from what she had seen of the female patients. Yes, she knew with each passing day she was more like them than daddy's little boy. This was when she learned to listen to the female patients, hoping to learn anything and all she could from them. Now she knows – she feels it, sees it. She is female, her blossoming bosom becoming more and more apparent with each passing day. Her manly parts never growing as Father had promised his young son. She had always wondered why "down there" had looked like all the female patients and nothing like the few male patients Father had. Father always promised soon, soon, he would grow and be a man, just like all other men. Then, she had believed. Now. Now she knew better. Now so much of the talk she had heard in the office was beginning to make sense.

With each new moment, she was more aware. She knew she was a woman. She was not daddy's little boy or this young son he was becoming so proud of. She had to talk to her father. He had to know. Yes, he had to know. He really already knew, didn't he?

She found him in his office where he spent all of his leisure time, which was anytime he was not in his operating room. For he was always busying himself with his books, either reading one or writing in one, always keeping track of every new experiment he had conducted and everything he had learned from them, making notes, writing all the information he could for her future use. Her reference books, he liked to call them. She felt she would never want or need any part of them. No, she did not want to grow up and be like Father.

As he looks up, she says, "Father, we must talk."

He smiles and says, "Come, son, sit. Have a seat."

"Father, that is just it, *I am not your son.* I am as female as the patients you have educated me with," she replies.

He shouts, "No, son! I told you, soon, soon you will grow. Soon you will be a full-grown man! A male, just as I have always promised. You are and will be my son, the son I have always wanted. You will be male, with patience and time and guidance from me."

She could not believe he would not listen to her, he would not hear her. Why? Why will he not let her explain? He has to know. She will make him listen. He will finally hear her! She shouts in a very angry and loud voice. As he looks up, she says, "No, Father, I am growing, but not into a male as you had always told and taught me I would, but into a female. I am growing female parts, not the male parts you need to be a man."

He replies, "No, I promise you. You will grow in the right ways to be just like me. A male. My son."

Again she pleads, "Father, I am becoming a woman. I need your help in becoming a woman. Father, please say you will help me. Father, I am so sorry I am not a son. I am not your son. I was born of my mother's womb a daughter, your daughter. Father, I am female."

"No, no, no. You are my son. I raised you, I made you. You are my son!" he shouted.

"No, Father, look for yourself." She rips open her shirt for her father to see that she is indeed a woman. "Yes, Father, I am a woman, a female, your daughter."

"No! Now cover yourself and be the man I taught you to be." He angrily storms out of the room and returns seconds later with a bandage, a huge roll of bandage. "Remove your shirt and wrap yourself tightly with this," he commanded. Saddened and hurt, she does as she is told. She cannot believe how strongly he objects. She has never seen her father so full of rage. He grabs her by the arm and drags her to the tower room and locks her inside, telling her she will stay there until she is ready to be a real man.

She sits crying day after day, with only her reflection to keep her company and the sight of her unforgiving father as he brings her a few scraps of food. What else can she do? She wonders. She is so lonely now, as she tries to be the woman she was born to be. A loneliness worse than that of living life as a son.

She wonders, to be a woman, what would it be like? What could it be like? Father was not a warm, loving type of person, never had been to her. He always seemed caring enough. She knew he had cared about her, at least as his son. Cared about his son. She knew she would have to try again. She knows it is almost lunchtime and he will be coming at any moment. She prepares herself to give this another try. She hopes she can make him understand, to make him recognize her for whom she really is and to still care for her. To have Father truly care for her and accept her for being herself was her greatest wish. Yes, this is what she must do.

She watches him as he enters the room. He looks tired and worn. His dull brown hair is a tangled mess. He has dark circles under his eyes. She can see by his appearance that this experience is no better for him than it is for her. The look on his rugged face tells her he is very displeased. He does not even acknowledge she is there or that she even exists at all.

He leaves her food and turns to leave.

"Father," she pleads, "I am becoming a woman. Please, Father, let me grow and learn to be a woman. Father, please accept me for the woman I am and will be. A woman, just like my mother. You married her. You must have loved her. She gave you me. Please!"

Father starts to walk away, glares back at her, and says, "That is why she is dead." Realizing her father's words, she falls into hysterical sobs.

Days pass. Not one word has been spoken between them. She wonders why and how could she want his love when now she hates him more than she ever thought it possible to hate one's father.

She decides to herself that none of this matters any longer. She sits herself up, looks at the image in the dusty old mirror. She stares long and hard at herself. She thinks. No one, nobody could ever tell she was a woman. She had no real features that even remotely resembled those of a woman's other than her now-bonded bosom. She looks so like her father. His eyes, his dull brown hair, his awkward height, even these fat fingers and large, wide feet. *What am I?* she wonders. No girlishness about her at all. Not in any way could she compare herself to any of Father's female patients. Why? Father, why? Father . . . I too she realizes, have been used as some kind of gruesome instrument in Father's experiments. He has tried in more ways than one to make me his son. She now remembers the medicines, the injections, and exercises – all of it was starting to make sense to her. This was the reason why her voice had been so much deeper than any of the other women that had come in to Father's office. She now knows that her whole life, Father was not only training her to be a son, his son, but was also altering her body's chemistry to assist him in his efforts.

The realization was making her mind reel. Her thoughts were so jumbled. She felt so lost, now more than ever before. Now, she was unsure of who she was, who she wants to be, or who she should be. Then she thinks, who or what can she be?

"Oh Mother. Poor Mother. How could he?" To her, he was nothing. Nothing but a cruel monster. Yes, thoughtless and cruel. She fully understands why she was never to see her mother. His whole purpose for Mother was now so clear.

Her tears fall down her cheeks.

"So sorry, Mother," she whispers. "Yes, so sorry."

CHAPTER
THREE

TO EXIST, TO be free, she must be what he wants. She must be his son. Yes, she decides; this is what she will do, for now. She thinks back . . . if they only knew. Ha, if she had only known. Indeed, she thought she did. She was just beginning to learn. She would be her own student. She would teach herself what she needed to know. Yes, somehow she would.

She could smell the aroma of the food as it wafted ahead to reach her before the food did. She hears him as he nears the door. She has herself dusted off and ready. Ready for Father. Ready to face him, to give him the news he had so dearly been waiting for. "Yes, Father. I am your son. I am the man to follow in your footsteps. I will do this proudly, Father, for you." They talk. Father is happy once again to have his son.

She feels a bit of relief knowing Father is once again happy. She knows she has to learn all that she can. This task would be easier for her being around the patients than being locked away. She decides, even if she has made a bad decision, to do her father's bidding, that maybe it will help her later in life when perhaps she will be free to be herself, be free of Father. Now she will have access to female patients again, only now, she will listen harder, pay very close attention to all they say and do, and even risk asking questions when she is unsure of what they may be talking about. She would have to hope they would say nothing to Father.

No, she was not happy with her decision, nor was she happy it had pleased him so much. She knew this must be done if she was ever to be who she wanted and needed to be. For now, she would endure and learn. She could cope with being Father's son awhile longer, she hoped. Father is excited.

He speaks of his plan to finish his experiment. He will have a son. She will be male. He has taught her in every medical field. He will now teach her his new surgical philosophy that will make her male. He tells her again, "I promised you would grow into a man. Now, we will make it happen, my dear son. You will be glad to be male and proud to be my son."

After hours and hours of explanations, demonstrations, and discussions about the surgery, the procedure, she recoils in defiance. "Father, I will continue to be your son, as I was before. I will continue to aid you, be your loyal assistant. I will even continue the masculinity medicines and treatments as you wish. I will never speak of this, I will never tell. Please, Father, do not ask this of me. Please do not surgically make me a male. Please do not make me undergo such a horrendous act. Father, I beg of you."

"I promised you. I promised you would become a man. A man has needs. You must do this to have and satisfy those needs. This must be done," he boomed.

She replies, "No, Father. I shall always stay here with you, only you. I will not have those needs. I will have you to care for. You will care for me. We will always have the patients. No, Father, I will not have those needs. Let me remain as I am, and I will do as I have promised. I cannot and will not allow or have this surgery you ask of me."

He reluctantly gives in and says, "All right, son. No surgery. You have been a good son. You have learned much, and you learn fast. You will do well. I will soon be assisting you. It is time you take over all main procedures."

Relieved, she agrees. She is ready for this next step in her life to get started and over with. Yet she is torn up inside to know she has once again pleased him.

Years and years have passed. Learning, cutting, experimenting, and operating... surgery after surgery... some failed, some ghoulish, some morbid and even fatal at times, but all taught and learned with greatness... perfecting explanations for both those who survived and those that did not.

She had kept her word to her father. She studied the human body inside and out, knew all he had taught her. She had become a perfectionist with a scalpel, cutting with the greatest precision, never missing her mark. So skilled. She had grown into such a fine man, such a great doctor. How could Father not be proud?

She had even quit thinking what it would be like to be a woman anymore. Now she had grown. She had become taller. Very tall. Her shoulders were broad and straight. Her physique looked a bit grotesque, but that no longer mattered. Her fingers were still fat but agile; her feet two sizes too large, she thought. Her face was a bit hairy in places, with a thickened chin. Her nose, yes, she thinks that could be that of a woman's. She had grown very strong. Her muscles showed through her sleeves, her legs long and fast. Yes, she had grown into a burly-looking man. Yes, she had become accustomed quite nicely to being Father's son, being content with who she was, with what she was.

But she had noticed, Father too was growing – growing old, growing feeble, not much of the man he once was, no longer able to stand tall and straight, eyes were squinting, and his voice was a thick whisper. This was no longer the man she had so feared. Still, he was a man proud to have a son. She often wondered about his father. Was Father the son he had wanted? What would his father think of him? What would his mother think of him? She thinks what a strange course that thoughts often take, reminding her of her own mother.

Mother, yes, poor dear Mother. No, you have not been forgotten. How could one forget such knowledge? Of knowing what one's own father had done to one's mother. Before this, she had never given it much thought, until the day Father mentioned why she had died. Couldn't miss someone you never knew. At least, this is how Father wanted her to think and feel. He had always said she should not ask questions that might make her sad. Sadness was a sign of weakness. No son of his would be weak. No, this was not acceptable.

Yes, she had put it out of her mind, till that day. Now she knew. She would never forget. This new knowledge had created new questions and feelings for her. Her mother's death now was not just being that of a horrible fate, one that separates mother and child, but one that was orchestrated by her father's own hand. She wondered even more what it would have been like to have had a mother – to grow with a mother's love, to be in a mother's presence, to have the admiration a mother bestows upon her child. To have her love, her help, her understanding, her guidance, and her protection – there were so many things she now realizes she had lost out on and missed as she never could have ever imagined she would. Yes, now she could only wonder. She would never know. Now she even wondered what she had looked like. Did she herself resemble her mother in any way? No, she was sure her mother must have been very pretty for Father to take her as a wife. She could only guess the kind of life she must have led with Father, the things she had to endure, to deal with. What she must have had to live with. Father and his high standards. Yes, she could now only imagine. Poor, poor Mother. She was very sad and sorrowful for her mother. She thinks, *If only I had been born a son, if only for Mother's sake*. Her thoughts make her very angry and outraged with Father. Still, an agreement was an agreement. She would not show any weakness or sadness in his presence. She was his son, a man of her word.

As the days passed, Father grew weaker and weaker, and soon became very ill. All their medical knowledge could not save him, could not help him.

In his last moments, she told him, "Father, I have been your son. I have been a good son. You have indeed taught me well. You have been a good father to your son. However, I will not and do not forgive you. I will no longer be your son, and I will not mourn for you. Instead, I will mourn my mother. I am her daughter. Good-bye, Father."

And she walked away, never looking back.

PART
TWO

CHAPTER
FOUR

OFF TO MAKE it on her own, finding what few pounds and coins Father had, she was on her way to a new life. She was ready to face this new world, to truly learn how to be a woman. A woman she could be proud of, a woman her mother would have been proud of. A mother's daughter. Daughter. Yes, now she could even be the daughter she was supposed to be. It was what and whom she was born to be. A daughter, she thought proudly. Mother's daughter. And she thinks what a relief to no longer have to be a son, a son she wasn't and didn't choose to be. The freedom to be exactly who and what she wants to be; the thought had delighted her so.

After many weeks of searching for a new home, she found a position as a nurse and housemaid with a young well-known doctor in the town of White Chapel. She had settled in nicely. How different this home was compared to the house she was raised in. It was more than she could have ever imagined. This was a home she could appreciate and marvel. Bright overhead lights without the glare, soft lights with high tones of colors throughout each room – there was a warmness about it, a warmness she had never known but gladly accepted. It seemed to have a life of its own, so light and lively. Every item of furniture was a true joy to look at, each chair or stool having actual-looking claws at the end of their legs, like those of an eagle, she thought. The shiny cherry wood glistened in the light. How wonderful everything looked.

She slowly walked from room to room, taking in each of the differences and beauty they all held. Filled with awe as she continued to wander about this house, she knew there was no doom and gloom here. She would make this her house. She knew this would always, from now on, be her home. Bursting with newfound joy, she knew she was going to be happy with this new life and this home she had found. Yes, she was going to be happy here. *Home* – even the word sounded sweeter and more inviting. *My home. My house.* Work was going just as well. The doctor had also created a very pleasant office. This too had soft light that poured in through the wide crystal-clean windows, light that made all the colors come to life. Upon entering the examining room, she was amazed. There was so much light. As she looked up to see a huge pane of glass for a ceiling, a roof, sunshine lighted every corner of this room. There was nothing cold about this room as it shone with bright sterile cleanness. She was going to love working here. She had surprised herself; there was a new word for her, one she hoped to use often. *Love.* Yes, this indeed was a new word.

The doctor often commented on her skills and was very impressed with her and her work. Of course, she knew she could be three times the doctor he was. This she would keep to herself. One thing she had learned from listening to the lady patients her father had was that men did not like it or think it possible for a woman to do a job better than a man himself could. There was a time she almost believed it. Almost.

She was becoming as impressed with the doctor as he was with her – not so much for his knowledge and skills, though they were of greatness, but more for his charm, grace, and very caring, tender ways with his patients. These were clearly not any practice her father would have used or possessed. This had enamored her to her very core. The woman inside of her was awaking. She wanted to be noticed by this doctor as more than his assistant, his nurse, or housekeeper. Yes, she wanted to be noticed as the woman she could feel herself budding into.

Thus far, the only way she had been able to get his attention was because of her skills, her professionalism. She would have to try harder. She would have to pay attention to his every wish, his every need at any time. He would learn how very thoughtful and helpful she could be. She would do all that it would take to make this doctor ever so happy.

She did this by always doing whatever he needed done whenever he needed it done. She would fetch this, go here, go there, run this errand, take this to, bring me this, get me that, clean this, scrub that – whatever he needed, that is what she would do. At work or at home, it would not matter. Yes, no matter what, for love. Her love, she hoped.

She was finally becoming the happy self she knew she could be. Life could be good, but there was still a twinge of regret for who she was. How she had wished she had not made the agreement with Father. Perhaps it would have been better to stay locked away until Father was dead.

It was hard to become a woman. It had taken a lot of practice to learn the graces and etiquette of a woman, all the new and different things and ways of her life in this new world of hers. All that her father had done to her made her work and goal so much harder to reach. Sadly, she knew there were some things she would never be able to change. He had made her "damaged goods." How she hated him, even more now than at the realization of her mother's death.

She remembers. She was once again a good student. She was excelling in the ways of womanhood. She was now indeed a woman, even though she did not look much like one. Yes, she could now dress in the finest dresses. She had even let her hair grow. It was long and shiny with a natural curl. She had a pretty face, with a boyish look to it. With time, hard work, and some medicines of her own, she had been able to overcome or change most of the male facial features produced by her father, only leaving a scarcely noticeable upper harelip. She thought her face still could be seen as slightly pretty, not a total loss. Her height, weight, and bone structure still showed her manliness. Her voice was still deep but not as bad as it once was. She had learned to use it in a burlesque way that seemed to work for her. She was somewhat content with herself. She only hoped she could make the doctor happy and content with her and her looks. She continued to cater to his every need and wish in hopes of making him happy with her doting ways. She was ecstatic when he had finally told her she was one woman in a million. He had noticed that she was indeed a woman. Now to get him to find her appealing, to get him to love her, to fall in love with her, he had to see she had so much more she could offer him.

She cooked him great meals. She cleaned fanatically. Each night after dinner, and during his baths, she would give him the most soothing body massages, gently caressing him in all the right places. Yes, he seemed to like her touch. The smile on his so handsome face told her he was pleased.

Her efforts were at last rewarded. One night after a great dinner, after making his bed and setting out his clothing, after drawing him a hot bath and having warmed towels ready for him, he enters the steamy, hot tub. She begins to massage him ever so gently, caressing his neck and back with the warm, wet cloth as she bathes him. His look, once again, tells her he is pleased and enjoying his bath very much. She is giddy from his pleasure. She finishes washing and massaging his arm that was closest to her; he smiles. She reaches over his relaxed body for the other arm. He grabs and pulls her in and passionately kisses her. She is so shocked. She jumps up and runs out without even kissing him back. She hears him chuckle as she rushes out. Now alone and wet, she thinks how foolish she had been. Foolish and stupid; after all, wasn't this what she so wanted? Saddened by the lost chance, she becomes afraid she may never get another. She realizes this was a moment of weakness. Weakness is not to be tolerated if she is to reach her goal. Father had taught her a few useful things; this was one of them. With this in mind, she straightens herself up and returns to the doctor's bedroom.

He is now lying on his bed. She hurries to his bedside and pleads with him to forgive her behavior, to accept her and allow her to return his kiss. He does. He takes her in his arms, and they kiss a very long kiss. She is elated. She now knows she can tell him how she really feels about him. How she wants to be more than his assistant, his nurse, and homemaker. She confesses her love for him with the hope that he too would someday love her. Perhaps they could make a life together. Without waiting for his response, she leaves his room.

The next morning, at breakfast, he smiles at her as he never has before. She is filled with hope and joy. Each passing day brings them closer and closer together. Their kinship blooms into a blissful romance. He formally courts her. They stroll together down the cobblestone streets. She is very proud and happy to be seen holding on to his arm. They go for rides to the countryside, have picnics, and take moonlit strolls. They are very happy together. All is in perfect harmony. They work together, live together, and love each other. She thinks all is great, life is great. Yes, she is woman. She knows it. He knows it.

CHAPTER
FIVE

S OON THEY ARE married and living as one and so very happy. She wonders, what would Father think? She usually does not allow herself to think about him. She, in fact, tries hard to not think about him. She wants him gone completely, even from her mind, her thoughts. It was just that she wanted him to know that yes, Father, she is a woman, a real woman. No matter how much he disliked the fact, regardless of all the things he had done to her, as hard as he tried to change her, she was now free. Free from him, free to be herself, free to be a daughter and, now finally, to be a wife. She felt so accomplished. She had overcome her overbearing father that wanted her as a son only. She became the daughter she was born to be, and now at last, the great joy of womanhood – to be a wife.

She felt she had become the happiest woman in the world. Finally being loved as a woman, she was beside herself with the delight of knowing she had all she ever hoped for and more than she could have ever dreamed of.

Life continues to be one of great wonder to her. This new life she had made for herself was becoming more joyful and exciting than she had ever imagined it could ever be. Her wonderful husband with his great dashing looks, whom any woman would be proud and honored to have; his so perfect face with soft curling lips that always showed a smile; a slim, short nose that just seemed to fit so well in the center of his unbearded face; best of all were his beautiful, piercing jade-colored eyes that seemed to shine with love and happiness.

She was still in awe to watch him deal with and care for his patients. He was so loving. He still commented and complimented her on her skills and abilities. Every day, they were learning from each other and about each other. The patients were very grateful they were a team and worked so well with each other. So in tune with one another, they would often say. It seemed one could not be without the other. Yes, they were a team, a very special loving couple. She knew she was as grateful as the patients were.

Life had so much to give and offer. They had already celebrated two wonderful and joyous anniversaries, two great and bliss-filled years as a wife. She would never forget she was indeed a woman, a very happy woman. With the arrival of their third anniversary, she was thrilled to announce that she was with child. He is happy. She is on top of the world, knowing that, of all the things she had done to be a woman, to become a woman, that this would definitely be the one thing that would certainly make her a whole woman. Yes, she was woman. She was with child, the ultimate joy and true fulfillment of womanhood. She was going to be a mother, she thinks, the final stage in her femaleness completed. Daughter, wife, mother – yes, she now felt complete. She was walking on air, so happy, so proud to be a woman. She thinks again of her father. She says aloud, "Father, I am with child. I am going to have a daughter or son of my own. I will love whichever it is. For me, it will not matter. But to have a son, a real son, would be such poetic justice. For me to have a son would be such a blessed gift. The gift you never had, could never have."

CHAPTER
SIX

A S HER CHILD grew inside her, so did the notion that something was awry. What should have been a time of blessed joy and excitement was more like doom and gloom. She was noticing that her sweet little paradise was soon becoming a place of loneliness. She felt she was losing it all when they should be at the peak of their happiness, having their child. She was, why wasn't he? Did he not want this wonderful child? Sometimes it seemed he barely even noticed her anymore. No kisses or hugs. No touches. No talks or walks. Why wasn't he happy? Did he no longer love her? Did he not want her? What was happening? So many questions, she thought. She did not like them. She must find the answers. She must make this better. She still loved him so much and wanted him to love her as he once had. Yes, she would find the answers. She wanted to be happy again. She wants her baby to be born happy and healthy. She wants her husband to be happy – happy with her, as she had always wanted and dreamed. This was the happy life she so longed for.

In her quest for answers, she sadly learns he is and has been having affairs. He has been seen with other women in dark alleys. How utterly horrid; and she thinks,

> I thought my life was full
> I had everything under control
> Now you have wronged me
> I did not want to see
> I tried to forget, pretend I did not care
> You continuously make me so very aware
> Yes, I do know
> And it hurts me so
> This pain should not be
> Oh, why can't you see?
> Because I love you
> I know what I must do
> I will let you back in
> So the healing can begin
> I know you truly care
> With your love to share
> This pain will end
> Our life will mend
> Together we will grow
> It will again be full.

Yes, the life she had always wanted could be just as she had always dreamed.

Days pass, and only a few flights of fancy does she get to spend with him. When she asks, he tells her he still loves her. So why? She can only wonder.

With only her unborn child being the true source of happiness, she goes on with her tasks at work and home.

Each new day, she hears more and more whispers behind her back. "Last night he was with Mary Anne" or "He was with Annie two nights ago" or "I hear he was with Liz last afternoon." All these whispers boomed loudly in her ears. Tearing at her very heart and soul, these names seared holes in her memory. Yes, they would be ingrained there. She would never forget them.

Still, she does her wifely duties; this is all it has come to mean to her. It once was love – a great love, so deep, so meaningful. They were once so fulfilled with each other. Now it was lonesome and tiresome. No longer does any love exist between them. It was all gone. It had disappeared along with her hopes and dreams. There was only angriness to clutch hold of and to cling to where her husband was concerned. He was making a mockery of her, of their marriage, and everyone knew it.

The angriness was building more and more each day. Now he too was laughing in her face, adding to the disgrace and shame she was already going through. How could she deal with this? How could she cope? He had become so uncaring, so cruel, afflicting such mental pain and anguish at every possible moment, having her when he pleased while bragging about whom he had recently been with. Mary Jane was his latest. He tells her he thinks he may even be in love with her. What a pretty girl she is. He was so blatant. How could he? Mary Jane. Yes, how could he? This name seemed worse than any of the others she had heard. This one seemed to mean a whole lot more to him. This one seemed to be special to him. Did he, perhaps, love her? What made Mary Jane more special to him? He had bragged she was pretty. He had never mentioned the looks of any of the other women.

No indeed, she would definitely never forget this name. How could she? Is she trying to take him away? No, she would not let that happen. Never. Was he trying to drive her out of her mind? Didn't he know she loved him as much as she ever had? She would fight for him, but she didn't know how to bring him back to her. Yes, she still loved him so much, and he continually hurts her. Why? Why? She wonders. She cannot understand how their beautiful love could turn into something so hurtful, unhappy, and ugly.

The one bit of beauty that remained of this love is this child still to be born. She must protect it and care for it. She loves this baby more than anything since he has turned his back on her. He needs and wants his ladies of the night. Yes, that is what he likes to call them. But she calls them what they are – prostitutes, nothing more, nothing less. Yes, she had noticed he suddenly had an increase of patients. He was bringing his ladies of the night into the office. Why? She wonders, wasn't the nights with them enough? The answer comes too soon for her. She realizes all too quickly just what it does mean.

He had done it – the last straw. He had given her syphilis. Hateful, spiteful man, she thinks. I could kill him. She hates him. She is going crazy out of her head with fear and tormented thoughts. Her worst fears had come true. She had such a severe case. She loses her sweet baby and can never have anymore. Grief-stricken, lonely, and half out of her mind, she can only think of the hate she feels. She has lost the one thing that meant the most to her, her only real love. Her baby. The chance to be a mother . . . gone. Gone. *Yes*, she thinks, *I will kill him*. She now hates him even more than she has ever hated her father. Her sorrow is so deep it feels like it cuts into her core. How does she go on? What can she do?

She knows what she must do. She must have revenge. Yes, she thinks, sweet revenge. Now it is all she can think about. With all this anger seething inside her, coursing through her veins. She knows how to do it. Father had taught her well.

He had come home for the day. She sees he too is quite ill. He asks for her help. She turns away. He pleads with her; he wants her to forgive him. He is so very sorry. She thinks it doesn't matter anymore. Everything is gone. You should be gone as well. She wants revenge, that's all. She now knows she doesn't need her plan. It will work itself out. Let him suffer. It is what he deserves. Yes, she will take care of him. After all, she is a nurse. They will think she did her best for him. Each day, he gets worse than the day before. He begs for help. She would only sit and watch. "You did this, you did this to all of us. Our child is gone, our love is gone. Everything is gone. Your love for me has been gone for a long time. But I loved you through it all and tried so to make this work, for us to be happy again. After everything now, my love for you is gone. I feel nothing but despise and total hatred for you. I cannot even stand to look at you. So no, I will not help you. To sit here and watch you die will be the only happiness I have felt in a very long time. It will give me contentment for my grief."

He gasps in disbelief. She sits. She watches. She waits. He is gone. She gets up and walks away. "Good-bye, husband, good-bye!"

She tried to care of herself. The disease was gradually getting worse. She was taking all the medicines she thought would help. They were somewhat helpful, though she did not know and could not be sure how much time she would have. She remembered when she had left Father's house.

She took very little with her, just things she was sure would be useful to her in finding her new life. She now remembers that one of those things she had taken was Father's book, with all his teachings and findings from his experiments written in it. She took it thinking someday it may be useful to her, even though she wanted nothing to remind her of him. But yes, this she thought she could use. She runs to find it. It has to have something in it that can help to make her better; at the very least, slow its progress. Yes, there it is; he had written a whole chapter on this. Most of his patients had suffered from this very same disease. How did she not know this? she wonders. He had indeed helped many. Treatments were mostly successful, over time.

Time. Yes, she hoped she had the time. She would gladly give her father's experiment a try. What did she have to lose? As she continues to read his book, she becomes shocked to find there is chapter after chapter about her, the experiments he had performed on her. These were all the things Father had done to her, all he had planned; step-by-step procedures; surgical, psychological, and physical instructions and demonstrations. "How dare he?" she shouts aloud.

As she reads on, she finds an odd, unbelievable ending to it. She begins to read it aloud. It read,

> I have found the perfect woman to mother a child for me. She seems to be a bit of a loner. She actually has no one. Her family is gone, died in some tragedy. She tried to tell me about it. I really wasn't interested. So, I do not know what happened. She is sad and lonely. With no one else in this world, she will come to love me, to trust me – me and only me. I will make her choose to spend her time with only me, to never wish to see another human.

She is stunned. Another entry reads,

> I am making great progress. She already adores the ground I walk on. She so cherishes me. Soon we shall be married. She is very anxious.

The next entry reads,

> We are married, she is pleased. She is a very good assistant. I think I shall miss her when she is gone.
>
> The goal has been accomplished. She is with child.
>
> She hopes for a girl, so do I. A boy would just ruin my plans. I would have to make it seem a stillborn, then start anew. That would take much-needed time. I would also have to keep the wife around longer than I had intended. No, if she has a boy, it just will not work out. She must have a girl. I need to have the child to be female.
>
> I will create a perfect son. I will shape him, mold him, make him. I will grow him, form him, and sculpture him. With my scalpel and my medicines, I will create the perfect son. He will obey and be at my beck and call and command and have the greatest respect and loyalty for his father. I will have a son, a father's son. He will be true only to me and will only be mine, to serve me and exist only for me, to continue on for me, and to follow in my footsteps as I have tried to do for my father. Only, I shall not fail. I will have the perfect son then do away with the mother. I have found her pretty and useful, but she would never agree or allow me to do this experiment. She would try to protect her child and even try to take it from me.
>
> No, this child will be mine, all mine. The mother would only be useless and in the way.
>
> She must have a daughter.
>
> It will be so tragic when everyone learns of how I had lost my precious wife, how desperately I struggled to save her life. They will know that I did and was able to save the child. That even through this great tragedy, I was able to bring a strong, healthy baby boy into the world. That I will care for and raise him alone. No one will ever know that she gave birth to a girl. Only I will ever know the true events. When the time comes, when she is ready to give birth to my child.
>
> How unfortunate it will be for her.
>
> Childbearing can sometimes be very fatal.
>
> The child will live and shall be mine.

A wave of nausea hit her. She could not believe what she had read. Realizing her father had actually wanted her to be born a girl so she could be his experiment from the start was more than she could handle. She was furious with all she had just learned. Being angered to her core stiffened her and somehow strengthened her.

Yes, she knew, now more than ever, she needed to heal, or at least somehow get better, to keep up her strength. So far, that had not been a concern. It was her grief that was making her go on. Her grief and anger. Now with her anger so much more intensified, she could only think of the revenge she so desperately wanted. Father was already gone. She could do nothing more to him except to continue hating him and being happy he was dead. Her husband was dead, a deed she wished she had committed but hadn't needed to. Yes, the hate she felt for him would be eternal as well.

She knew these were not the only two people in the world that had caused her torment and pain. There were others that had caused her great pain as well. Yes, she fully knew he was not the only one that had caused her to lose her precious baby, her greatest joy, her last remaining reason to live. The wonderful life she had once had was ruined and gone because of him and his creatures of the night who were always making themselves available to him. Yes, they were to blame too. She now had a new reason for living, to live. She wanted revenge, and revenge she would get. She did not care if it took her till the end of her time; she would not rest until she got her revenge.

She had not forgotten one single name. She could still hear all the whispers of the patients buzzing in her ears. She could hear his mocking laughter. All the memories just fed her angriness. She certainly would never forget Mary Jane!

Yes, she thinks she will make Mary Jane suffer. She will make her feel all the pain she had caused her to feel. Yes, it will be painful. She will hurt. Mary Jane had taken her husband's love for her away. Yes, she is the one who had caused me the most grief and pain. She is the one who gave me my greatest sorrow. Yes. Indeed, she will pay.

She was grateful that Father's treatment had been working. With each new day, the symptoms seemed to lessen. Yes, she could feel she was getting better. She knew that as long as she kept with what she remembered reading in the steps for the cure, she would be well in a matter of months. Father had actually done something great with all his experimenting, but no one will ever know what he had done, what he had discovered. No, no one will ever know of his cure, this cure. She had been so upset with what he had written about his plans for her. In a fit of rage, she had shredded every page of his book and then tossed the torn pieces in the fireplace. As she watched them burn, she sadly thought that perhaps, if she had remembered having the book sooner, it may have saved her baby too.

Now, she was once again strong and capable. She was ready for her revenge. She would have a plan of her own. She would get satisfaction. How sweet it will be to make them suffer, as they had made me. Yes, all of them. Indeed, they will regret the day they interfered in my life, with my life. They took my life. She would wait as long as it would take. She has nothing left but time. Yes, she thinks, she will get her revenge. It will be fulfilled. Anger and rage flow through her, giving her a renewed sense of resentment and grief.

Yes, this deed must be done for me, my baby, and my husband, for the life we did not get to have. Yes. Indeed, I know who they are, and I will find each and every one of them. I will make them sorry they ever touched my wonderful husband. I will make them sorry they were women.

After many days and many nights, weeks that turned into months, months that turned into years, I found them all. Yes, even pretty Mary Jane. I made them all very sorry, sorry they took what was mine. I took what was theirs. Yes, when I was done with them, I had indeed made them sorry they were women.

Father taught me. Yes, Father taught me well.

For I am now known as . . . Jack the Ripper.

Edwards Brothers,Inc!
Thorofare, NJ 08086
14 July, 2010
BA2010195